Mala

A women's folktale

adapted by Gita Wolf

illustrated by
Annouchka Galouchko

Annick Press Ltd.
Toronto • New York

One summer day, three gypsy women came singing and dancing into Meena's village. They appeared suddenly out of the hot dust like bright birds. On their heads were baskets full of puppets and in their hands lutes and tom-toms, as they sang:

Hear our tale, women
Hear our tale, children
Hear about the demon
Who swallowed the rain

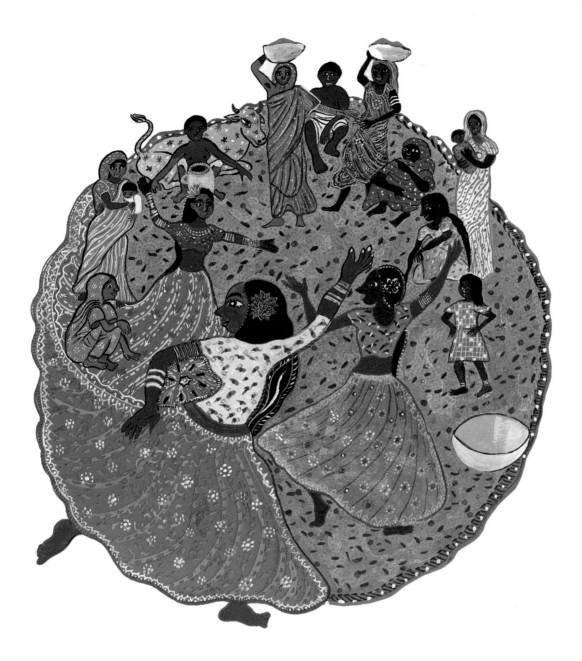

The women and girls dropped their work to listen: the gypsies could tell wonderful stories, clever and wise, and it was said that their women possessed magical powers.

In Meena's village it had not rained that year. The fields were barren, the riverbed dry. Every day the girls walked many miles for a pot of water.

When the gypsies sang of the demon who swallowed the rain, the women came out of their houses to listen. Little children stopped playing and the bigger boys dropped their books. A large crowd surrounded the gypsies.

We will tell you the story of the demon and the rain seed. And of a girl—why, just like this one here! Yes, you, *cried the gypsies and pointed straight at Meena, who laughed with delight. The gypsies continued:*

There was once a girl called Mala, with shining eyes and lovely black hair. She and her brother, Mani, lived with their family in a small village in a faraway land. A mighty king reigned over it in great pomp and splendour.

Mala's home, like all the others in her village, was a tiny hut and without comforts. Mala helped with the household chores. She would have loved to learn to read and write, like her brother Mani and the other boys in the village. But there was so much work to be done every day! Life was hard, year in, year out.

And then things became worse: there was not a single drop of rain in the land, month after month.

The King called his clever Minister to him and asked, "Why is there such a drought?"

"Because, Your Majesty," answered the Minister, "a terrible demon has swallowed our rain seed. There will be no rain until it is planted in our land."

"Call out the Army!" ordered the King. "This cannot
be allowed!"

So the King sent a mighty army to fight the demon and
bring back the rain seed. But not one soldier returned.

Then he called for the tallest, strongest and bravest men in
the land. Some went to the demon on foot, some rode horses,
and some even rode elephants. Not one came back.

He sent out messengers with huge drums to every corner
of his kingdom. They shouted, "Hear ye! Hear ye! A
message from the King: the man who slays the demon and
brings back the rain seed shall receive half the gold in the
treasury and half the kingdom!"

Mala's brother was ready to try. But the King began to laugh when he saw him. "Such a young boy—what makes you think you can kill a demon?"

"I am known for my bravery," Mani boasted. "When I was only a year old, I put my hand into a snake hole and caught a snake. At two I tamed a wild buffalo. And when I was three, I killed a tiger that had terrorized three villages. Allow me to try, O King!"

The King was unconvinced. Then the Minister slid up and whispered in his ear, "We don't know, do we, which snake lurks in which hole...? Likewise, Your Majesty, who knows what good may come of this strange lad's claims? Let him try! If he succeeds, we get rain. If not..."

And so Mani set out to defeat the demon.

He never returned, and Mala and her mother were heartbroken.

One day Mala sat for a long time at the water hole. "I wish I knew what to do," she thought. She closed her eyes, and when she opened them again, three smiling women stood before her.

"Oh! Who are you?" Mala exclaimed.

"We are your godmothers. What can we do for you?"

"Mothers, do tell me when my brother will return!"

"Mani? The demon has turned him into stone."

"Is there no way to save him?"

"There is. You must kill the demon, rescue Mani and bring back the rain seed."

"You are teasing me," said Mala, "how can I do that?"

And she ran away. On the long walk home, she began to think about what her godmothers had said. Face the demon? By herself? ...Then she became very excited.

"Mother, Mother! I want to rescue Mani and fetch the rain seed!" she cried, entering their hut.

"Are you out of your mind?" scolded her mother. "Should I lose you too? You are only a girl. Stop this silly talk at once!"

Mala could hardly hold back her tears. She dropped her water pot and ran out of the house.

She ran and ran like a desert wind and only stopped when the village was far behind her. Then she sat down under a thorn bush. "Only a girl!" She had had enough. She did all the housework, the cooking, the cleaning... She was really angry, but she didn't know what to do. At times like these, there was nothing in the world she wished more than to be a boy.

To hold back her tears, she shut her eyes very tightly. She saw her godmothers and heard their words. She stood up and walked briskly to the King's palace.

"Stop!" said the guard. "Where are you going?"

"I want to see the King," said Mala boldly, and marched right past the guard.

"What might you want, little girl?" asked the surprised King.

"I have come here because I want to go and find the demon. I want to rescue my brother and bring the rain seed back to our land."

The King laughed. So did the Minister. They laughed and laughed. Finally, the King wiped the tears from his eyes and gasped, "This is a real demon, little girl, that you are planning to kill. Not a doll. To tame him, you need strength and bravery."

"I have all that," said Mala confidently. "I go all alone through the countryside at noon to fetch a heavy pot of water. I go all alone to the forest to gather firewood. I do all the housework."

The King became serious. "These things all girls do. Now go. A little girl setting out to defeat a demon, indeed!"

Mala left the palace in tears. How she wished she were a boy! She closed her eyes and willed her godmothers to come to her.

"Don't cry, little one," they said, appearing before her. "Why do you want to be a boy?"

"Because," sobbed Mala, "I want to fight the demon. Everyone says that girls are good only for housework. I want to be a boy! How else can I kill the demon?"

"There are many ways. We will grant you your wish. But we may not change you back. You will have to do that yourself."

"All right," said Mala slowly.

"You might not like being a boy."

"Why not?" said Mala excitedly. "Imagine being a boy at last! I can do everything I want! But I don't know where the demon lives."

"We will show you the way, but you cannot call us anymore. You will have to manage all by yourself. Do you agree?"

"I agree! I agree!" shouted Mala, "please let me be a boy!"

Mala's godmothers covered her with a piece of bright cloth. They then began to chant and dance around her. When they removed the cloth, there was a boy called Amal!

Mala's godmothers gave him a mirror, saying, "Amal, you have the arts of a boy. Learn to use them wisely. Look into this mirror when you need help. You will see Mala. Now we will show you the way to the demon."

The demon's land was eerie and desolate, full of huge rocks in strange shapes. The only living things were the vultures, slowly circling in the sky. Amal skipped along, whistling. Then, all of a sudden, he saw an old woman sitting on a rock, mumbling to herself.

"Water, water," she moaned.

"Hey, old woman! What are you doing here?" demanded Amal.

"Oh my child, I'm so thirsty. Please give me water, bless you."

"Grandma," said Amal, "don't worry. I'm off to bring rain to the whole land. Let me pass."

The old woman blocked Amal's path. "Get me water first," she demanded.

"Hey! What is this? I have important work to do. Let me go!"

"Water first."

Amal looked around. Where was he to find water in this godforsaken desert?

Suddenly he thought of his mirror. He saw Mala, whose voice said to him, "Amal, look for a cactus. There is water inside."

Amal was relieved. "Oh, all right! I'll get you water," he said, and hurried off to find a cactus.

When he came back, the old woman had vanished without a trace! A hoarse voice cackled, "All right, go on. You are a clever boy. But too proud!"

Amal looked into his mirror. Mala's voice said, "It must have been the demon in disguise. But even so, I didn't like the way you talked to the old woman."

"But Mani always talks like that! Boys do."

"Nonsense. I wouldn't have thought that a boy has to behave like that, just because he is a boy."

Amal walked on. He saw a dog standing in his path, an ordinary, scraggly little street dog. Without thinking, Amal lifted a stick to chase it away. He raised his hand—and his stick disappeared! Amal stood still with shock. Then he took out his mirror for help. Mala's voice said, "What did you do that for? What did the dog do to you?"

"It's the only way to deal with these filthy creatures. Mani would have done the same."

"How silly! What would you have done if this mirror had disappeared too? You have to be careful. I must say that it is difficult being a boy. Imagine having to do things like that all the time! Now we have to go on."

As Mala's voice said these words, there was a sound of laughter. Amal crept on, over the boulders and rocks. The laughter became louder and louder.

—And all of a
sudden, there was
the demon, right in
front of him.
You can't begin to
imagine how
terrible the demon
looked. Amal stood
completely still.

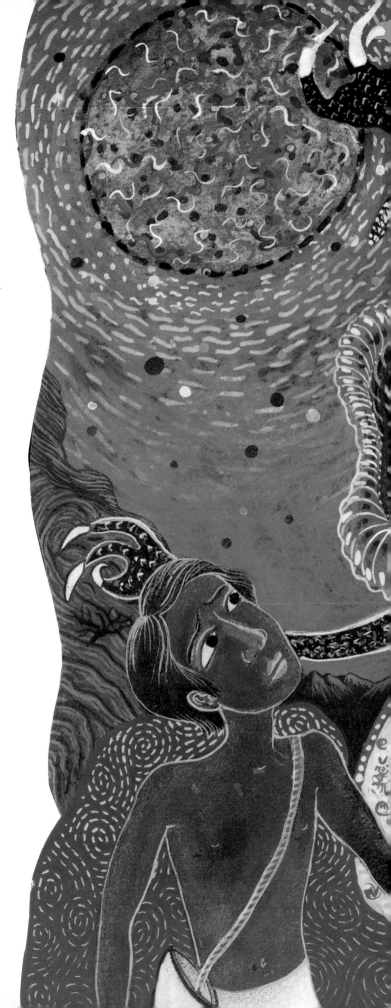

"Ho, ho, little boy!" the demon bellowed. "Come on, come closer. You are the only one left in your land, eh? So you have managed to come so far!"

"I've come to take back the rain seed," said Amal in a small voice.

The demon laughed loudly. "The rain seed, indeed! Ha, ha! Do you know how many strong men have come on that mission? And how many have succeeded? You have to defeat me first!"

"Ye-es," whispered Amal, trembling.

"What!" shouted the demon, "you little shrimp! To defeat me you need to answer three riddles, or I'll turn you into ashes!

"Here is the first. It has three eyes, but is not the god Shiva. It has hair all over its body, but is not a bear. It has a tuft, but is not a monk. What is it?"

Amal stood speechless. He did not know.

"Go on, answer me!"

Amal peeped into the mirror hidden in his hand. Mala's voice whispered to him, "A coconut, silly."

"Oh, that. It's a coconut," said Amal, casually.

The demon sprang back in surprise.

"Correct. But now the next riddle: what has four legs in the morning, two at noon and three in the evening?"

Amal scratched his head. Then he peered into the mirror.

This time, Mala's voice spoke out loudly: "That's easy! It is a human being! Early on, we crawl on all fours. When grown we walk on two legs. And in the evening of life, we need a stick as a third leg."

As Mala's voice said this, the mirror fell from Amal's hand and broke. For a moment the world turned upside down, and in that instant Amal turned into Mala once more. You should have seen the demon's face! He was speechless with horror. "A girl!" he whispered in a hoarse voice, "a girl! I have never fought a girl before. This is cheating! Fraud! Deceit!"

Mala took a step toward him. He backed away in fright. Mala laughed. "I'm not afraid of you! I've come this far using my own wits. Go on! Ask me your final riddle!"

The demon managed to stammer, "W-what is r-red, becomes black and then turns grey? If you don't have the answer," he said, with some of his old spirit, "I'll turn you into ashes!"

But Mala was not to be frightened. "It's firewood," she said confidently. "I know it so well."

As she said this, a huge flame engulfed the demon. He turned into ashes, right in front of Mala's eyes. And in these ashes Mala spotted a large, juicy seed. As she picked it up, her brother Mani appeared.

"Mani, Mani, here is the rain seed!" she said excitedly.

"Well done, Mala. You should really have been a boy!"

"No, I shouldn't!" said Mala hotly. "I'm proud of myself. I defeated the demon, didn't I? Using all that I have learned as a girl? I knew all the things Amal didn't."

Then Mani put the rain seed into his pocket and said, "Come, let's go to the King."

They reached the palace surrounded by a large crowd of people. The King appeared and saw the rain seed in Mani's hand. He said, "We are pleased that the rain seed was saved. Minister, arrange for this brave lad to plant the seed!"

Mala was speechless. Mani put the rain seed into the ground. Everyone looked expectantly at the sky. "Where is the rain?" murmured the crowd.

"There is something wrong. The seed hasn't brought rain."

Mala didn't know what to do. She didn't want to shame Mani in front of everyone. She closed her eyes and called her godmothers. They appeared and announced, "There will be rain when the person who defeated the demon plants the seed."

"Mani, didn't *you* kill the demon?" demanded the King.

"No," said Mani quietly, "it was Mala. I'm sorry."

Mala took the rain seed and put it into the ground. She carefully patted earth over it. As she did so, huge black clouds appeared in the sky. There was a thunderclap. And down came the rain in a great gush! The crowd cheered. And the King proclaimed, "You, Mala, will receive half the gold in my treasury and half the kingdom."

The Minister drew him aside and said, "Your Majesty, can she rule over a kingdom? Would it not be enough just to give her the gold?"

But the King had learnt his lesson. "A person who can defeat a demon by herself," he stated firmly, "is capable of ruling a kingdom. Mala will receive everything I promised."

You should have seen the rejoicing!

And that is the story of Mala and the rain seed, *cried the gypsies to their audience in Meena's village*. Everywhere, at all times, there are Malas, and may the rains come for you too! *And Meena, who sat right in front, looked at them with shining eyes and a wide smile.*

Canadian Cataloguing in Publication Data

Wolf, Gita
    Mala

Adapted from the film Girija by Madhyam, based on a traditional Indian folktale.
Originally published under title: Mala : a women's folktale.

ISBN 1-55037-491-5 (bound)   ISBN 1-55037-490-7 (pbk.)

I. Gravel Galouchko, Annouchka, 1960-
II. Title. III. Title: Girija [Motion picture].

PZ7.W82Ma 1996   j823   C96-930223-1

The art in this book was rendered in gouache.
The text was typeset in Oranda.

Distributed in Canada by:
Firefly Books Ltd.
3680 Victoria Park Avenue
Willowdale, ON
M2H 3K1

Published in the U.S.A. by Annick Press (U.S.) Ltd.
Distributed in the U.S.A. by:
Firefly Books (U.S.) Inc.
P.O. Box 1338
Ellicott Station
Buffalo, NY 14205

Printed and bound in Canada
by Quebecor